TALES OF THE TITANIC
by *Michael Trelissic*

copyright 2014 Michael Trelissic. All rights reserved

I wish to record my thanks to the members of the Tuesday Writing Group for their help and encouragement.

This book is a work of fiction, although the story of the Titanic is real and a matter of public record. Names, characters, businesses, organisations, places and events are either the product of the authors imagination or are used fictitiously. Any resemblance to actual persons, living or dead is entirely coincidental.

I wish to dedicate this little book to my grandmother

Mary Ann Craig – nee Kelly

1886 -1971

who travelled to America as a young woman at about the same time as the Titanic sailed, to work in service. She subsequently returned to England to marry my grandfather John Craig and had nine children and many grandchildren, one of whom was me.

The story of the Royal Mail Ship Titanic is true and a matter of public record.

Over 1,500 lives were lost when the Titanic, thought by many to be unsinkable, went down in the near mid Atlantic during the early hours of Monday 15th April 1912.

There were 2,200 passengers and crew on board but there were only 1,200 places on the lifeboats. In spite of this 500 places remained unfilled.

Titanic 1 Joseph and Alice

Down in steerage the noise from the revolutions of the giant steam driven engines was constant. Men coughed and spat, infants cried and women hummed familiar tunes to their infants to bring on sleep. Alice cuddled closer to her Joseph, slipped her arm more securely into his and sliding under their blanket she closed her eyes. Joseph thought of how he missed his mother and widowed grandmother, unsure if he would ever see them again. Thank God I've no children, he thought. It was one thing to be hungry yourself but he was not going to suffer the pain of watching his children go hungry, not like his brother and two sisters. In the darkness he heard the occasional cry of a baby and the distant chime of the ship's bells over the constant sound of the engines.

Joseph considered himself lucky to have been given the casual work in the vast kitchens, earning a few pounds to add to their meagre savings of £13.17s.3d with which to start their new life in America. The kitchen was the source of everyone's food, where each potato was the same as every other potato. The food had equality, at least until it was served up. Then patterned plates and silver cutlery distinguished the first class potato from the steerage class potato, served directly onto the passenger's own bowl with a ladle. Joseph knew about potatoes.

"Yes you, come here. Get changed and report to the dining room on A deck. Look lively now." a junior officer commanded. Joseph was surprised and nervous. The urgency of the order allowed him no time to tell Alice, before climbing upward through the decks passing through the class system of the Georgian age. When he entered the unfamiliar world of first class the sight before him came as a shock. Never had he seen so many toffs in one place. Keeping as close as he could to the vast dining room walls he made his way slowly around to the service hatches on the far side. The scene was very different from dinner in steerage; the diners were so clean and upright. He had never before seen a lady without a hat and here there were hundreds. Monochrome films at the penny picture house had

never hinted at the array of colours and scents that were laid out before him.

"Steward, you steward." The voice broke his trance and demanded a response; an elderly lady sat opposite a young woman at a nearby table for two. The young lady looked sad, her pale face contrasted with the red of her hair. Her eyelashes curled upwards, revealing a pair of large green eyes which sparkled like the emerald necklace that lay heavily on her white neck.

"Are you alright?" asked the elderly chaperone.

"Yes" stammered Joseph.

"Bring me a jug of iced water."

"Yes, yes" replied Joseph, still unable to divert his gaze from the young lady.

"Quickly, quickly."

Joseph nodded respectfully. As he straightened he noticed the young lady smile at him, a smile that turned his legs to jelly and his mind to a state of ecstasy and wonder.

"You must be Scanlon" said a chef emerging from behind the steam of boiling pots. Joseph nodded.

"You do not, repeat, do not, report to the kitchen through the dining room. That is for first class passengers and first class waiting staff only."

"Yes, sorry sir, I lost my way."

"Far end, through the galley doors", pointed the large figure.

The rest of the evening of Sunday 14th April 1912 was busy, very busy. The steam rising from the enormous sinks suggested that, after a brief glimpse of heaven, he was now paying for his sin of desire in hell. After a nervous start he settled into the routine of washing up, thinking of the beautiful girl, when he suddenly remembered the order for iced water. The plate slipped from his grasp and exploded onto the floor. Joseph crouched to collect the pieces before being discovered. Too late, a voice pierced the steam

"That will come out of your pay."

Joseph binned the pieces noticing the broken crest of the White Star Liner, Titanic. He couldn't wait for his shift to end, so he could tell his Alice of the amazing sights he had seen. But he decided not to mention the girl. Stupid of him, he would never get the chance to even speak to her, let alone form a relationship. Perhaps one day, a long way off, people like him would have a chance with people like her. His mind wondered back to the family home and the violence shown to them all, particularly his poor mother. The man from Derry who came to our town in secret and spoke in hushed tones offered a way to channel these feelings and many eagerly took up the cause. But that was not for him, warned his mother. "You must go son, take Alice and go to America." Wiping a tear from his eye he realised there were no more dishes and the galley was now quiet. Making his way to the dining room he looked at the now empty table for two and sighed. She'd be getting ready for bed in her first class cabin, perhaps having a hot glass of milk before slipping between clean sheets. Guilt abruptly broke into his dream as he thought of Alice.

The night air was cold on the open deck as he started down the metal stairways. He was pleased, if a little puzzled, to hear the distant sounds of the band playing Nearer My God to Thee. Still thinking of the beautiful young lady he was not braced for the collision with the Iceberg and so, when the great ship shuddered from its mortal wound, he was thrown forward and fell down the last three steps onto C deck. As he pulled himself up by the rail he heard the sound of the rending of metal and shouts of alarm from below. As he hurried downwards his progress was soon blocked as frightened passengers filled the stairways on their way to the boat deck. Appeals from the loudspeakers only served to increase the pressure of bodies. There was now little hope of Joseph being able to reunite with his beloved Alice. It was not the religious divide which now threatened their union, it was death. The river of humanity continued its slow progress upwards. Joseph managed to stay on his feet but had to grapple with the hand rail as the ship dipped a further five degrees and an ominous rumble was heard from below. The ship's incline and the rumbling noise was accompanied by further cries of alarm. As Joseph steadied himself with one hand, he used the other to grab a boy of about three as he was about to be crushed from behind. Holding the boy tight in one arm he held onto the rail and slowly made his way at last to the boat deck. Ice from the open deck spilled down the staircase and many slipped. As they did so they grasped at anything they could which was often another equally terrified passenger.

The sheer number of people on the open boat deck prevented progress very far from the top of the stairs. The new sound of lifeboats being hoisted and lowered increased the pressure from behind. A shouted order was repeated and rolled over the crowded deck

"Women and children first, women and children first."

The order had a calming effect and the crush eased a little. The majority of those in his view were first and second class passengers who could be distinguished by their attire. The boy looked around frantically from his elevated position in Joseph's arms. His expression revealed his dismay at not locating his parents.

"They'll be along in a minute, don't fret now." offered Joseph in as confident manner as he could muster. People were now praying openly, some sobbed softly and the band played on from somewhere on the deck below. Families were preparing to be separated and wondered if they were to be parted forever.

"Women and children first." came the order again.

"I knew this was an unlucky ship." murmured a rough looking man who seemed to be the worse for drink. He reminded Joseph of his father and his violent reaction when he found out about Alice.

Joseph was torn. Could he hand this child to another whilst he searched for Alice? The decision was made for him as he turned and looked back down the stairway from which they had just emerged. It was crammed full. With a leaden heart he slowly scanned the scene before him and stopped as he studied a lifeboat suspended, before being swung over the side .The women and children aboard looked at their husbands, fathers and sons for the last time. He admired those brave men who stood quietly accepting their fate so that their loved ones could live on. Two women had to be physically parted from their husbands and were pushed aboard. It was then that Joseph resolved to save the boy.

"What's your name son?"

"My name is Randolph." replied the boy, in his cultured English accent.

"Listen Randolph," responded Joseph in his soft Irish accent.

"I want you to be really brave and make your ma and da proud of you. Put your arms around me neck and hold on as though the devil himself is after us. See that boat hangin there, I'm goin to get you onit." Joseph pushed, squeezed and riddled his way through the crowds shouting

"Make way, make way, child coming through, make way." The crowd parted like the Red Sea but his progress was eventually halted about six feet from the lifeboat. The ropes had taken the strain. His progress was blocked by three men of enormous build who were dressed in identical blue serge suits, white collars, and black trilbies.

"Take the boy." Joseph shouted as he hoisted Randolph above his head and then lied, "His mother is on board." The men turned to face him. Their features identified them as identical triplets. Six enormous hands stretched over the heads of the people. Randolph was lifted by one of the hands and swung through the air and received by outstretched, willing hands on the small craft. The young women who received the child looked at Joseph. It was the lady with the red hair and emerald eyes. He'd been right; she had been getting ready for bed, confirmed by the dressing gown she was now wearing. He could just make out the features of her face from the ship's lights; her body profiled against the star filled sky showed she had donned her lifejacket. As she took the child in her arms the hoist resumed.

For a moment the young woman and the boy stared down at Joseph's uplifted face, as high above, another distress flare burst in the night sky.

Many years later, Joseph could still bring to mind crystal clear images of that night. It was only after the last lifeboat had left and the shout of "Every man for himself." was heard that he jumped into the freezing waters and struck out.

Climbing onto an overturned collapsible boat he was sure he would be sucked down with the great ship but a half empty lifeboat returned and picked him up.

Incredibly, he was reunited with Alice in New York a week later. It seemed she had come looking for him when he had failed to return to her an hour after the expected time. She was only two decks below the boat deck when the ship was struck and she was able to board one of the first lifeboats to leave.

Joseph married Alice in a civil ceremony and went on to do well as a union official in the construction industry. It was only when he felt secure that he had children. He named his first son Randolph. Joseph never gave Alice a reason for not attending the annual reunions of the survivors of the Titanic.

Titanic 2   The Teachers

Tom glanced once more at his second-class ticket and allowed himself to remember how proud his mother had been when he gained his first teaching appointment. He had attended the same school and so had his mother Margaret before him. Now he was returning as a qualified teacher of class four at Saint Marie's Junior School.

The new head, Mr Walsh had given him the usual talk. "Make them work hard Mr. Connor, and don't put up with any nonsense. Here is your cane." he bellowed as he swished it through the air with a sadistic look in his eyes. "Make sure you use it regularly, Mr. Connor, it will drive out the devil from the little urchins."

As a pupil Tom had only received kindness from Mr Doyle the previous head. It was largely due to him that he was able to pursue his chosen career. He had shed a tear when he heard of his death and offered a prayer for the repose of his soul.

Miss Sarah Craig occupied the adjacent classroom teaching class three. Tom regularly stole a look at her through the half-glazed wall when he thought his class wouldn't notice. They always did, signalled by their giggles. Sarah was as graceful as she was beautiful and had been appointed a year earlier. She hated giving out the cane, made obvious by the lack of force behind the strokes, but the head had insisted that she cane three boys in the morning and three in the afternoon. He would often visit her class and leer over her before picking out three boys, seemingly at random, for the ritual punishment which he would administer himself with abnormal delight.

Tom and Sarah were attracted to each other from the moment they met in the staff room at lunchtime. A procession of year four boys brought the teachers' lunch from the school kitchen, two hundred yards away from the school itself. The first boy through the door would always scan the room for Mr Walsh, and then proceed accordingly with utmost care if he were present. Following on, Sarah always sat next to Tom if the lead boy sighed with relief and didn't if he didn't.

Over the months Tom learned that Sarah was an only child like himself. Both fathers had died in the Boer war leaving their widowed mothers to bring them up. Sarah's family had been relatively well off and could manage without an income from her while she was at college. It had been very different for Tom whose mother was virtually destitute when her husband failed to return from the war. She had taken the infant Tom and returned to her mother's terraced house built by the Mill owners. She worked very long hours at the mill to keep body and soul together. It was due to the compassion and generosity of one of the many priests that Tom was able to go to college. Father McKenna was a young Scottish Priest who had recognised Tom's ability at school and opened doors for him. His mother cried when he left but only when she had waived him off and closed the door. Another bout of coughing left a trace of blood on her sleeve and confirmed that the consumption was taking hold. Tom shed many tears at his mother's bedside as she slipped away. She had waited for his return from college. He would never forget the look of fear on her face as he drew the threadbare sheet over her sightless eyes. Before she had let go she held her beloved son's hand and looking into his eyes, had smiled. Her last words were "Look after yourself son. I'm so proud of you."

It took Tom and Sarah a year of teaching to save enough money to buy their tickets to start a new life in America. Sarah's mother had died six months earlier. Sarah had been left £200; all that was left of her mother's estate after her debts had been paid. Tom had about £30 after he had paid for his ticket. His mother had nothing to leave, not even the money to bury her. Tom made sure this was the first debt to be settled when he received his salary.

Tom left Saint Marie's school under a cloud. He had suppressed his disgust and anger at the head's cruelty to the children but it boiled over on the day Patrick Donnelly became the latest victim of the sadist head. He had been late for school and stood there, the rain dripping from his dirty shirt onto his bare feet. He tried to explain that he was late because his father had been taken into hospital but the head didn't give him a chance and laid into the boy with a fury that even surprised Tom who had witnessed many previous beatings. Patrick was one of Sarah's pupils and it was her cries of "Stop it, stop it you brute" that made him break off his teaching and look through the adjoining window. Sarah had grasped the arm of the head as he was about to bring the cane down on the poor wretch once more. The head pushed her aside causing her to fall to the floor as he cursed her. Tom flew out of the class into the adjacent room and smacked the head on the jaw with his fist, which sent him sprawling onto the front desk causing the inkwell to jump from its casing and send its contents into the air. The ink-spattered head exploded with rage and sacked them both on the spot.

Sarah appeared from the bedroom of their second-class cabin and put her arms around Tom from behind as he sat on an upright chair still fingering the White Star tickets. This awoke him from his thoughts about the recent past. They had been married the week before and Father McKenna officiated. Only two other people attended, Samuel and Iris, friends from college. Father McKenna's gifts to the happy couple were glowing testimonials, which he handed to them, as they left his church for the last time.

They had travelled down to Southampton on the first of the transatlantic trains from London Waterloo. Their first sight of the Titanic took their breath away. She was magnificent; her four gleaming stacks towered over the docks. Sarah clapped her hands in glee and turned to look into the eyes of her beloved Tom.

She had seen the reflection of the great ship in his green eyes and thought their futures looked equally grand. Tom laughed and drew Sarah to him contrasting his grey overcoat with her blue winter coat, his black hair with her chestnut brown which tumbled halfway down her back.

Dinner was a grand affair, consisting of eight courses. Although Tom's wardrobe was modest, Sarah had a different dress for each evening and on the first night she wore her spring colours of pastel green and blue. She looked every inch the English Rose. Tom wore his wedding suit of navy blue serge, white starched collar and shirt and his college tie. Class wasn't important to Sarah but to Tom it was relevant, remembering the poverty he was born into. Their days on board were happy and consisted of strolls around the magnificent decks, elongated meals and talk of their future together in America. This was most intense at dinner when their surroundings became almost opaque, they were so engrossed. This was different from their first evening; when Tom had scanned the full dining room and unconsciously arranged all the diners into a hierarchy, from those who he thought had just scraped into second class to those who were pushing the boundaries of first class.

 The collision with the iceberg shook Tom from his dream. Although he felt no more than a jolt, it frightened him as memories of his fragile happiness once before flooded into his dream. The loss of his mother had taught him not to be too happy, it could all be shattered in an instant, like the crystal bowl he had once seen smash into a million pieces when an unfortunate little boy had knocked it from its display in the newly opened departmental store in Manchester. Taking Sarah by the hand, Tom hurriedly made his way to their cabin and enquired of passing crew if there was any danger. They all reassured him that there was no danger but to listen for any announcements. Sarah attempted to calm Tom as she saw his panic rising but Tom's feeling of dread from his past experiences could not be suppressed. Pulling on his life jacket he urged Sarah to hurry and only take their money and papers including the precious references. His urgency increased as the announcements started. "Would all passengers make their way to the boat deck? Would all passengers make their way to the boat deck?" Again Sarah tried to calm her husband but to no avail. Tom, now wild eyed held his wife's hand in an iron grip and only eased it when Sarah cried out in pain. Standing firm she slapped Tom's face, which was now contorted with anguish and fear.

"Tom, Tom you must calm yourself." she cried and then kissed his cheek. "There is no panic. We shall proceed calmly. Come." This approach had worked with her pupils and it worked again with Tom. Taking his hand she made their way along the corridor, which was now filling with frightened passengers. There was no panic, just the sounds of anxious parents hurrying their children along. Progress became slower and slower as they made their way onto the remaining second class deck and then the first class decks as more and more passengers filtered into the main stream of passengers all heading up to the boat deck. Sarah and Tom's arrival onto the open deck was met with shouted orders from the officers "Women and children to the boats, women and children only."

Sarah felt the cold air hit her as she looked with dismay at the packed crowds between them and the boats, the first of which were being hoisted ready to be swung over the side. As the announcements registered with Tom "Women and children only." his grip tightened once more and he put more effort into pushing through the crowd. As Sarah allowed herself to be pulled along she focused on three huge men, one of whom was\swinging a young boy over the heads of the crowd to the outstretched hands of a beautiful young women in the boat that was being hoisted aloft. Now afraid of falling and being trampled Sarah managed to free herself from Tom's grip but before she could re engage she was swirled along as though caught in the current of a fast flowing river, and was carried away from her husband towards the railings of the deck. Abstractly she wondered at the vastness of the star filled sky and felt completely calm. She had never seen the night sky so clearly, the smog filled skies of her hometown had always hidden the incredible beauty above. Having no control over her movements she was carried along until she became aware of a crewmember that lifted her hand, and with his back pressing against the crowd, was able to assist her into the last remaining seat in the lifeboat. As she allowed herself to be seated her silent trance ended and she became aware of the many sounds around her. Husbands shouted farewells to their wives and children, sons bid farewell to their mothers, and fathers their daughters but as the boat was hoisted, she saw that most were silent, only their eyes taking their last longing look at their beloveds in the knowledge they would never see them again. A tear welled as she marvelled at their bravery and a silent prayer passed through her lips to be manifested into a mist, by the cold air, as it slowly rose to begin its journey to the heavens.

Over the sound of the clanging chains of the hoists a cry came from the deck below. "Sarah, Sarah I love you." It was Tom's voice. A light from a distress flare lit the crowd below and she found Tom's uplifted face. He appeared calm and deliberate and strangely serene even though he was jostled on all sides. "I release you Sarah, I release you. Be happy for us, be happy my love." Tom only relaxed his gaze after the lifeboat was lowered over the side.

Sarah decided to stay in America and settled in a small town in Virginia where she became a dedicated and highly valued teacher. She brought up her son Tom there, whom she was unaware she had been carrying the last time she saw her beloved husband. Tom never tired of hearing about his brave father who was afraid of nothing on the face of the earth.

Titanic 3: Mary Ann Craig

Mary Ann was the third of 14 children of Albert and Margaret Kelly and they all lived in a two bed roomed terraced house in the mill town of Oldham, Lancashire. Mary Ann, or Annie as she was known left school at 12 as did her best friend Bella or Isabella, as she insisted on being called, when the mood took her. The year was 1907 when they entered the mill and 1912 when they left. This was not for them. They had discussed their plans to go to America at every opportunity which included miming over the noise of the giant looms. Annie's family did little to dissuade her as they wanted better for her even though they would miss the wage she brought in. "Don't worry Mama, I'll send what I can." Annie had said. Bella's mother had a younger sister who had recently returned from service in the southern states and it was she who had secured employment for the young girls. Annie remembered well the day the letter came from America confirming their appointments in the household of Bertram Squires, the owner of a large estate in South Carolina. The envelope also contained third class tickets for passage to New York aboard the new White Star liner Titanic. Annie's blue eyes sparkled as she read the letter time after time and her chest inflated and deflated rapidly as the reality sunk in that this was real. She was going to America.

Bella sat opposite Annie after the sight of their families waving goodbye was hidden by the steam from the train as it pulled out of Manchester. They were quiet for a time as they reflected on what they had left behind and the massive adventure they were embarking on. There had been boys back home, many more had pursued the beautiful Annie than the plain Bella but Annie was not going down the road their mothers had; worn out and old before their time. Unknown to Annie, Bella had given in to a boy who had been rebuffed by Annie. She had thought that this was one the few chances she was ever going to get and later had persuaded herself that her morning sickness was due to nothing more than the excitement of her new life.

Two days later as the girls were taking in the view from the port side of the mighty Titanic, as it steamed away from Southampton docks, they were alarmed at the near collision with another, much smaller ship, the drifting liner New York. A deck hand, smitten with Annie, inflated of chest and exaggerated of rank, rushed to reassure the girls that there was no danger, after all, their vessel was the largest in the world and virtually unsinkable. As was usual, Bella took second place in the flirting and silently began to worry that her nausea might not be entirely due to the rolling sea. Annie used her charm to persuade Jack, the deckhand, to take them on short and secret tours of the upper decks, to marvel at the grand dining rooms of second class and the immaculate dining rooms of first class before returning to the noisy and uncabined floor of steerage. On the second day out the girls befriended an Irish girl by the name of Alice. Her husband had gained temporary employment in the kitchens and she was left for many hours on her own. His return was celebrated with a selection of savouries retrieved from the left overs of the upper class diners, which the girls were happy to share in. This was the first friendship the girls had made with someone from outside their Lancashire culture and they embraced the experience. They soon found that apart from their accents they had a lot in common, most notably the distance between their Christian faiths and poverty of the populations.

During the late afternoon of the third day, Sunday 14th April, Jack turned up and invited the girls to go on another excursion through the ship. Alice declined fearing repercussions on Jack's employment should they be caught? Bella complained of seasickness and also declined.

  Annie, wide eyed, took in all the sights and the hours flew. This would be her one day, sailing second class with her American husband on a return trip to Lancashire to visit her family.

"Can I help you miss?" asked a smart young man who had noticed her staring at him and his wife."

"No sir, sorry I was just taking the air, daydreaming."

"I see by your accent you are a fellow Lancastrian" returned the young wife.

"Why yes, Oldham. Do you know it?

"A little, it was nearby I went to teacher training college."

"You're a teacher." said Annie, with undisguised admiration.

"We both are." said the young man as they walked on. "Have a good trip."

As the couples parted Annie swung around and said "Oh Jack, I'd love to be a teacher."

"You can be anything you want to be in America." he smiled a loving gaze, not fully realising that he had just fallen in love. "

Come, the suns been down for hours and it's getting chilly, I'll take you back."

Before he could turn towards the stairs the ship shuddered and Jack caught Annie as she fell towards him.

"Oh Jack, what was that?"

"Probably hit a piece of driftwood, nothing to worry about, I'm sure. You make your way back and I'll go and find out."

Annie was about to make her way back when Bella and Alice emerged from the stairs. Alice explained that she was in search of Joseph who was two hours overdue so they had made their way up the decks together.

"Would all passengers make their way to the boat deck. Would all passengers make their way to the boat deck." came the first call over the loud speakers. Although worried by this announcement the girls didn't voice their fears but continued their way in silence up the stairs and accepted lifebelts handed out by a crewmember. When they arrived the boat deck was wide and almost empty. Crewmembers were manning the ropes and pulleys of the lifeboats. Annie felt a chill as the announcements continued. Bella gripped Annie's arm and shivered. Alice cried and said Joseph's name wishing him to appear.

"Over here miss" shouted a deckhand holding on to a rope as a lifeboat was lowered.

All three looked across in a daze.

"Quickly, it's going to get very busy here soon." he shouted.

As if they had been waiting for permission, bewildered passengers started to flood onto the deck. Annie looked down to see twin girls aged about four being ushered forward by a smartly dressed woman with an American accent who asked Bella to look after them saying she would be right back. Before she could respond the woman disappeared back down the stairs and was quickly swallowed up in the now thickening crowds. The girls stood there ground wondering what to do as the crowds now flowed passed them like a river swirling around half submerged rocks.

"Where's mama?" asked one of the twins confirming the woman's identity.

Annie as usual took charge of the situation and told Bella and Alice to get to the boats; she would wait for the twins' mother. After their protests were waved, Bella and Alice made their way slowly through the crush across the open deck to the lifeboats.

Precious time was spent waiting. "Where was she, how could she leave her children."

As though the children had read Annie's thoughts one of them said that mama had forgotten her pretty things. Daddy would be cross if she lost them.

"Women and children only" came the latest chilling announcement.

"Madam, please take your children to the boats." ordered an officer who had just arrived on deck. The great ship started to list.

"Oh they're not my." Annie's voice faded as she saw her friends on a boat being hoisted. They were shouting, she could guess what, but couldn't hear their words above the commotion.

The deck was now full and more people were trying to crush their way up the stairs.

Annie was now shivering almost uncontrollably as a man shouted

"Repent, repent the Lord is punishing you for your pride. Unsinkable you boasted. The Lord speaks but you ignore Him at your Peril."

These words made Annie doubt her sanity but then she felt strong hands grip her shoulders from behind. It was Jack. She turned to face him as a distress flare lit up the sky behind her, lighting up his face. He was calm and assured and she felt an immediate calm. Taking one child each into their arms, Jack led the way through the throngs towards the last remaining boats shouting "Children coming through." In spite of her returning fears Annie was in awe of the frightened men, who despite the fear written on their faces gave way in almost total silence to allow them through. She had been persuaded to wait no longer for the sake of the children and nearly tripped over a man kneeling before a priest who was giving him absolution. The children were lifted into the boat and then Annie turned and paused to thank Jack. She was profoundly moved to see tears rolling down his illuminated face. As she was lifted up, she held his gaze.

"Jack, thank you, thank you. I'll never forget you." They both knew this was a final goodbye and that they would never see each other again.

As the last of the boats rowed away from the stricken ship Annie tried very hard to reassure the children that their mother would be on another boat and that they would see her soon. The Titanic, all its lights blazing sparkled in the clear night air as she imagined a palace would look like. Suddenly the great lady of the sea dipped steeply into the smooth sea, seemingly accepting her fate like the graceful lady she was. Would this atonement wipe away her sin of pride? Annie drew the children to her breast as she stared over their heads at the ship as it slid under the waves. The steam from the stacks met the water with a mighty roar, which she was grateful for, as it muted the screams of the condemned. The sea was silent for a long time afterwards until the cries of those in the water carried across to those in the boats. Some half empty, turned back to help but most didn't, fearing they would be swamped. Annie's boat was full so thankfully the decision was made for them.

Annie was reunited with her friend Bella in New York a week later. After the initial euphoria of their reunion, Bella's eyes questioned who the man was that accompanied her.

"Oh this is James Madden, the father of the children we helped onto the boats. He has offered us accommodation until we recover and can continue our journey to the South."

Bella knew at that moment, as she met his Madden's eyes, that this would never happen and that she was about to lose her beloved friend Annie who would replace the mother who was lost; and so it proved to be.

Bella was invited to the wedding a year later but had already left for home in Lancashire without her baby daughter Beatrice, who lay in the ground of South Carolina, a victim of diphtheria. Annie and Bella exchanged letters over the next couple of years. In her first letter, Bella told the only other person who would ever know the truth. This was the first Annie knew of the pregnancy and who the father was. Annie regretted telling Bella of her happiness at her own pregnancy in her first letter and about the nursery that was being prepared.

Many years later Annie and her family of four children visited her family back home in Oldham. Bella had married and was expecting her eighth child and looked pale and worn out like their mothers had been. On the eve of her departure back to America, Annie was finally able to speak to Bella alone. They were very different people now but, for a few precious moments, they were young carefree girls again. They laughed until Annie told Bella of how Jack had rescued her and the children and how in that last moment of parting they had lived their lives to the full, and they wept.

As Bella closed the sticking door behind the last of her children to re-enter the terraced two bed roomed house, she found an envelope on the bare table. It had her name on it.

Titanic 4   Father Harold Williams

Father Harold boarded The Titanic at Southampton and although booked into a second class cabin he chose to give it to a young family from steerage and to take their place on the open third class accommodation. As a newly ordained young priest he was full of fervour for his ministry and wanted to practice humility and love for his fellow man. His spiritual director at the at the Seminary had advised him not to rush things: better to slow release his love and compassion than let it all out at once and exhaust his reserves, after all his training had been long and expensive and he was a valuable church asset and he should not take risks. Whilst his faith in God's protection was admirable, he should not put the Lord to the test too often, like the time he threw himself into the path of a runaway horse to save a young child who had wondered into the crazed animal's path. Thinking back, he hadn't thought about the possible consequences of his actions but he wished the thought of caution hadn't been put into his mind, because if there were a next time, he might hesitate and regret it later.

During his seven years at the seminary his only contact with the opposite sex was on the odd occasion he was allowed to go to Mass in the nearby village. When he entered the seminary, at the age of twelve, girls hadn't interested him in that way, but at the age of 19 they were a source of improper thoughts which his confessor had warned him about often and given him the example of Eve who was the downfall of Adam and many since.

On his regular strolls around the upper decks he saw many beautiful young women; thankfully they were accompanied by their husbands or vigilant chaperones. His priest's collar was his pass to all decks and his background and education equipped him with an air of confidence which was never challenged. On one such excursion he met the family he had given his cabin to; they were carrying their belongings in a couple of hessian sacks and were heading down to steerage. When questioned they explained that they had had enough of being ignored and abused by both fellow passengers and crew and would be far happier with their own kind. Reluctantly Father Harold relinquished his halo and remembered how vigorously his parents had adhered to the class system. Initially they were pleased that their second son had been called to join the church but were horrified when they realised that he meant the Catholic Church. This would not do; how would they explain this to of their Church of England friends. In a way they told the truth when they said he had gone abroad.

He was still carrying his smile when his eyes met those of an unaccompanied young woman. Regaining his composure he tipped his hat and continued past her although her beauty was impressed on his mind. Unable to restrain his temptation for a second look he turned, only to see her also turn. This was a sin, so nervously tipping his hat once more, he continued on his way feeling the heat from his blushing face.

Kneeling by his bed to say his night prayers Father Harold repeatedly tried to summon the vision of the crucified Christ but only saw the beautiful face of the young woman. The night seemed endless as he drifted in and out of sleep as he continued to be tormented by intruding sinful thoughts.

Breakfast in the second class dining room was a splendid and long affair. He was grateful for the distraction of fellow passengers taking their seats at table. Father Harold had been shown to a table for two on the edge of the dining room. His fellow diners consisted mainly of families and elderly couples and the noise level increased as more passengers arrived. Next to his table was another table for two but it remained vacant. The waiters became increasingly busy, coming and going, coming and going and the scene became a blur as he went through the motions of polite exchanges with people passing, coming and going. Having finished his breakfast and about to leave, a frail, elderly lady accompanied by an attentive young woman were shown to the next table. After carefully seating her charge the young lady sat and looking up, noticed Harold and smiled. He nodded in acknowledgement and desperately hoped he wasn't blushing again but the heat of his face told him he was. It was the same young lady whose face had haunted him all last night. Calling silently for God to help him he hurriedly left, quickly tipping his hat.

Alone in his cabin Father Harold knelt by his bed and again asked God to help him. He recalled the day of his ordination. It was an extremely solemn affair lasting from early morning to early evening. Together with two hundred other young men he swore allegiance to God and to no other. In his address the Archbishop had warned them that the devil takes many forms including that of attractive young women and that they should be vigilant at all times. Once they had set their hand to the plough they must never withdraw it under pain of damnation. Their vow of celibacy carried similar warnings should they fail and he recalled a moments hesitation when his turn came to take the oath. The celebrations afterwards were lavish and although comparatively brief it seemed an age to Harold. He felt awkward and out of place as he was the only new priest who had no guests. His sister had promised to attend but a last minute intervention by his parents had put paid to that.

Harold spent the whole of that day and following night on his knees drifting in and out of sleep. He asked if he would always have this mental tormentor or if, in time, it would relent and allow him to give himself completely to his calling. In the early morning, exhausted, he fell asleep.
In what seemed less than a heartbeat there was a knock on his cabin door. The knock was repeated several times, each with added urgency until Harold dragged himself up and answered the door. It was a steward who, after apologising for the intrusion, informed the priest that his presence was required

as an elderly lady had fallen ill and had requested him to attend. Splashing his face with cold water he glanced at the mirror. His handsome, young face peered back through half closed eyes showing the fatigue he felt. Clutching his small sacramental bag, he hurriedly followed the steward up a deck to a cabin on the port side. Thanking God for this diversion he was shaken when the door was answered by her. His guilt flooded back into his bewildered head and he wondered if the thorn in the side of Saint Paul had been a beautiful young woman. He failed to hear what she said until she repeated herself. "It's my aunt, please come quickly."

The aunt appeared to be unconscious. The doctor shook his head slowly in the direction of the young lady as he vacated the chair to allow the young priest to sit.

"It was aunt's wish to receive the last rites of the church." explained the young lady tearfully to Father Harold. Opening his bag he withdrew a small white linen cloth and placed it carefully on the bedside cabinet. Onto this he reverently placed the holy oils and holy water and a small silver candle holder. Having lit the candle he opened his missal and administered the last rites. Inviting the young lady to join him in the final prayer he asked their names. "Elsie Father, Elsie Turner. My aunt's name is Mary Turner, she never married."

This was the first time Father Harold had administered this sacrament and although it was a sad occasion, it felt good, very good. During the following days he counselled Elsie and so accompanied her to all meals and spent all his waking time with her. Elsie told him that her aunt was her last relative and that she was now completely alone in this world. They got to know each other intimately and Harold was grateful to share his recent life with her and was on the verge of telling her of his recent turmoil but he didn't have to, she had guessed at it and felt her own rising feelings for him. On the third night of their acquaintance Harold arrived for dinner wearing a tie and not his clerical collar. Elsie, of course, noticed but said nothing; she was bewildered with her own mixed feelings of love, grief, guilt and shame. Fellow diners had noticed their growing attraction for each other and spoke in whispers about this scandalous affair, she just bereaved, he a church minister. Not Church of England, thank God, but never the less a minister of a church. But the couple were oblivious; theirs was such an overwhelming feeling that could not be resisted. Not even the unspoken threat of eternal damnation was going to keep them apart.

When it came, the collision was the bolt from Heaven that Father Harold had feared. He must bear the greater guilt; he was the priest, she a vulnerable young woman who had just lost her only relative, her only source of security in this world.

"Women and children only." came the cry on the crowded boat deck. Elsie was scared, so was Harold who vowed to get her to the boats.

"No, no", she protested," "I'll not leave without you."

"I have work to do, I'll join you as soon as I can." he promised, as he struggled to don his clerical collar. Elsie took hold and gently fitted his collar as a loving wife may have done as she looked into his watering green eyes. He returned her loving gaze and saw she was also weeping. A tug on his jacket from below broke the spell, a young man was kneeling before him.

"Father, will you hear my confession?" he implored.

A sailor's firm hand took hold of Elsie's arm and pulled her towards the ladder to the boat. Harold looked across as Elsie took her seat. He then turned to the penitent and holding his hand over the poor man's head, gave him absolution. The officer in charge of the boat shouted. "Father, there is a place left. Will you take it?"

Elsie looked down at Harold as the priest looked up; he was now surrounded by a circle of men of all ages, two deep, all kneeling before him. His face answered her question. He was no longer anguished or fearful, he was serene. He was fulfilling his calling, what he had been called to do, and he, like the penitents kneeling before him, had already accepted their fate. Raising his hand he gave them collective absolution, as he was empowered to do. He then turned and gave the sign of absolution to Elsie as the boat was hoisted out of sight and over the side.

Elsie returned to England and took up residence in her aunt's house in Dorset. As she started her lifetime of mourning, she wrote to the Archbishop and gave him an account of Father Harold's bravery and dedication to his office to the last. She asked him to send a copy of her account, without mentioning her, to Father Harold's parents. In addition to the house, Elsie's aunt left her a small annuity which was enough for her to live a modest lifestyle. She was offered marriage a number of times but declined with thanks. In this way she would atone and perhaps meet her beloved once more on the other side, where they would be together for ever.

Titanic 5   David Jones

Life in the Boiler Room was noisy, dusty and very hot. About the best that could be said was that it was better than being down the pit but the big attraction was that at the end of his first voyage he was going to see New York. He, David Jones, was going to America.

The chief stoker abruptly broke into his dream saying the captain wanted more speed and to increase the shovelling rate. It was true then; they were going for the record, for the fastest Trans Atlantic crossing. That'll be something to tell his mates back home in the Valleys but now his biggest problem was keeping the sweat out of his eyes. Stripped to the waist like all the stokers, David was wet through when the evening shift relieved them. Showers were knew and much easier than the tin bath in front of the fire in the cramped living room of mam's house. Everything about his life was new since he and his best friend Harry had joined the White Star Line and left the poverty and endless misery behind them. Their new jobs weren't by any means cushy numbers but it was so different and life now had so much promise. The food was on board amazing, there was so much of it and the quality was so much better than they had been so used to. A stroll along the outside steerage decks after their shift was the highlight of their day and flirting with unfamiliar single girls along the way was a new and thrilling experience and made them feel truly free unlike their friends and family back home for whom their was no escape from the grinding poverty. On one such occasion they joined in conversation with two Irish girls of their age and had their first kiss. Harry teased David about him bending his right leg backwards as he kissed his girl. "Isn't it the girl who's supposed to do that?" he joked as he ran from the scene, hotly pursued by his friend.

Their next shift was the evening shift, starting at 20.00 hours on Sunday 14th April and due to go through the night until 06.00 the next day. Both David and Harry, whilst not exactly liking their work, relished the thought of feeding those enormous boilers, which were the lifeblood of the ship and which seemed to have a life of their own. Both men had seen their mothers' spoon-feed their younger siblings and it seemed that they were spoon feeding a giant alien creature with an insatiable appetite that roared its thanks, but then immediately demanded more as every shovel full of coal was thrown into its fiery mouth. Entertaining these thoughts the time went quickly and the shift was almost half over when an ear-splitting wrench of tearing metal tore through the boiler room and stunned the men. A rush of water and shouts of men was heard coming from the direction of the adjacent boiler room.

The two stokers looked to the chief to answer their unspoken questions but for a moment everyone just stood there as if frozen to the spot. The order to stop engines was heard over the speaker, which shook the men back to life. David looked at his friend Harry and Harry looked back through his coal dust covered eyelids. David looked perplexed rather than worried. What was happening? What had invaded their world, their new world where bad things didn't happen?

Bad things only happened in their old world like when another infant died or there was a blast or flood down the pit. Things like that didn't happen in this newly discovered world of theirs. As water started to tip over the bulkhead from the adjoining boiler room the chief stoker shouted "Right lads off you go but stand by for orders when the engineers sort this out." Mr Bradley, the chief stoker sounded different, like a sergeant major might sound before the battle, caring like, as though he knew that things were bad but were going to get a lot worse; David thought he sounded like the pit manager had when he announced to the waiting wives and children that there was a roof collapse in the main shaft.

The two friends climbed the metal stairs of the boiler room as sea water rushed around their legs and pursued them all the way up the narrow stairs. Cries of help were heard from below as they reached the hatch to the lower deck, the water now only feet from them. As they emerged Mr Bradley battened down the hatch trapping a number of screaming men below. The protests from the two were answered by the chief who said "Orders lads, orders, we can't risk the ship being swamped." his face was contorted with grief as he continued. "The ship is going down lads. All the bulk heads are the same, as one fills, it overflows into the next and so on until the ship tips forward and goes down. Get yourselves up to the boat deck and save yourselves."

In shock and still not knowing what had caused the mighty Titanic to be holed, the two friends from the Welsh Valleys raced to their quarters and picked up their few belongings. As they climbed the stairs to the upper decks they were amazed to see that life was going on as normal as it was before the collision, passengers were still in the dining rooms having their evening meals, others were strolling along the decks. As they started their way up to the first class decks they were challenged by an officer. "Hey there, you two, what are you doing up here?"

"Don't you know the ship is sinking, doesn't anyone know?" stammered Harry. His words were overheard by several passengers who gathered around.

"That's nonsense," the officer replied "We had a brush with an ice- berg, that's all, nothing to worry about." he addressed the passengers who now numbered about twenty. He was about to continue when the loudspeaker burst into life.

"The ship has been in a collision with an iceberg and as a precaution passengers are advised to put on their lifejackets and proceed to the boat deck."

The message was repeated as the passengers started to retreat to their cabins and the two friends continued on their way, their faces now strained with worry.

"We'd have been safer down the bloody pit." ventured Harry as they stopped to help the two Irish girls they had met the night before put on their life jackets.

"I can't swim." admitted David as they escorted the girls along.

"No need to worry" offered the auburn haired Kathleen. " We'll all get into the same boat. It'll be nice and cosy." she said as she linked David and smiled at her friend.

"To be sure." agreed her brunette friend Marie as she in her turn linked Harry.

As though the devil had been eavesdropping the loudspeaker boomed "Women and children to the boats, women and children only."

"Oh Jesus." gasped Kathleen, "It's real, we are feckin sinking. Oh holy mother of God." she blasphemed as she released her linked arm, as though abandoning David to his fate.

"It's just a courtesy" said the more controlled Marie. "They just mean women and children first, then the men."

"I'm not so sure." said the increasingly worried David. "There doesn't seem to be enough boats to me."

"That's because this ship is supposed to be unsinkable." agreed Harry.

"Unsinkable my arse." spat out Kathleen. "Why are we tilting then? Come on Marie lets get to the boats." she urged as she dragged her friend along, almost falling over a man kneeling before a young priest.

David and Harry watched the girls go as crowds of people pushed and jostled from behind. David didn't like crowds; it made him feel insecure, probably because he was nearly trampled once by the Welsh rugby crowd when their team beat England in Cardiff. A choir started up, reminding the lads of home and the unique feeling of belonging as the men of the pits sang in the clubhouse on a Saturday night. They might have been poor but they belonged and they looked out for each other and shared their lives, the brief glimpses of joy amid the multitudes of sorrow. David recalled seeing his father's death certificate stating the cause of death, written by a weary Welsh doctor "Worn Out, poverty". Staring into the clear starlit sky and wiping the tear that had formed he mustered his friend.

"Come on Harry lad, we're not finished yet, grab those life jackets." he nodded in the direction of a deck hand carrying a whole load of them.

Staring ahead the friends looked at a boat that was being hoisted and smiled as they saw the two Irish girls on board. Kathleen was fussing with her few belongings whilst Marie searched the scene below until she found the boys and waved.

"You always did attract the right kind of girl Harry." offered his friend longingly.

"It's funny David, it's as though I have known her all my life."

As another flare exploded in the cold night sky the ship dipped once more causing the crowds on the deck to call out in fear.

"Remember how we lashed those logs together to make a raft on the river Harry. Well, let's get to it. Those curtain poles in the dining room and the cords."

David's eyes sparkled half with anticipation and half with a desperate hope as they struggled against the prevailing crowd.

The two men made their raft, their life raft and launched it as the ocean gently swept over the bow of the great ship. The cords held and the fragile craft bore their weight with ease. They even managed to drag a young priest aboard but finding he was dead, let him fall back into the sea. Using two chair legs as improvised oars they drew away from the ship before it could drag them down with it. The raft stayed afloat long enough for them to be picked up by one of the few rescue ships.

When news of the boys reached the valleys the two boys were hailed as local heroes and the male voice choir sang about their two sons of Wales with pride.

In New York Harry met up with Marie in the clearing sheds and they eventually married and settled outside the city. He survived the Great War unlike many of his friends from the valleys. Kathleen got in with a bad lot and ended up on the streets and was strangled by a drunken client on a cold November night in 1914. After two failed relationships, David returned to the valleys and married a girl he had gone to school with. She had been widowed by the war, like many others. David took on her two young children and reluctantly returned to the pits where he dreamed about those few, precious days on the Titanic and of what could have been.

Titanic 6 : The Celts

Garret had never before left the island of his birth, situated off the North West coast of Scotland, in all his 80 years. He now found himself on the mighty Titanic heading for America .His grandson and interpreter Benedict accompanied him. They were to be the guests of an American senator who had traced his ancestors to the neighbouring Scottish Isle and wanted to know more about his roots.

Garret was a Celtic priest. Although the majority of celts had embraced Christianity, some had clung onto the old ways and regarded the earth and all its creatures as sacred and the property, not of man but of divine forces. His priestly office had required him to receive and learn by heart the old laws and sacred texts and to pass them on orally, nothing was to be written. Now in an unfamiliar world he was unwilling to be contaminated by his surroundings. Unable to tolerate or cope with this modern world the priest rarely left his cabin, even taking his meals there. In the small hours Garret would emerge alone on deck and stare for long periods at the sky and the sea and quietly incant an ancient ritual. From the other side of the ship he could be caught in tall profile, his arms outstretched in the moonlight. His appearance might have alarmed the modern traveller sporting as he did a wild unkempt shock of hair and beard, and his eyes penetrated as though he could see one's soul. As the wind caught his loose robe, a tattoo of a white unicorn was revealed across his chest. It seemed to move as the moonlight caught it and then a passing cloud hid it for a moment. A pendant of blue stone set in pewter flashed as the moonlight returned and matched the rich blue of his eyes. As the dawn started to break behind the ship the old celt returned to his cabin. A report filed by one of the night look outs included an account of what looked like a dark figure leaning over the port side of the ship and then moved along the deck as though floating. His superior made him scrub this section of the report on the grounds that the captain might think he had been drinking.

The priest's grandson was baptised with the Christian name of Benedict on the insistence of his mother who joined the island community when she married Garret's son. It had been a happy union but she kept her husband's family at arms length as she always felt uneasy in their presence, especially Benedict's grandfather. They never spoke directly to each other as Garret spoke no English although she suspected that he did, but chose not to use it, preferring to speak in Gaelic. It was her that saw to it that her son received a conventional education, not wanting him to remain on the edge of society which many of the pure bred celts chose to, influenced by their priests and culture. So she had sent her son to the mainland to be educated under the guiding hand of her brother, a minister of the Church of Scotland. However during the holidays he spent much of his time with his celtic grandfather and a strong bond grew between them. Benedict reassured his mother that he was not being groomed or initiated into the old ways and that his love for his grandfather was nothing to be worried about. Over the years he had become fluent in Gaelic and enjoyed the tales and music of old which were celebrated at the regular gatherings of the island community. Benedict's mother, Margaret noticed that new blood was brought in from the mainland for such occasions and soon realised that it was only the sons who brought in and married the women. She never saw or heard of any men being chosen as husbands for the local's daughters. This would account for the many spinsters on the island. On the only occasion she brought up the subject with her husband he evaded the question saying she was now part of the community and shouldn't question their practices; she might give the impression that she didn't wish to stay.

Fearing that her husband might try to keep her son on the island she didn't object to her son accompanying his grandfather on his trip to America. It would broaden his horizons and allow him to see the opportunities in life. This would further her secret plan made with her brother for Benedict to study medicine in Edinburgh on his return. He would be the only male in living memory to leave the island permanently.

On the afternoon of Sunday 14th April, the day of the collision, Benedict dressed in a tweed jacket and a kilt played the bag pipes in an impromptu concert on the first class deck, much to the delight of the passengers, especially the Scots. His grandfather had asked him to play an ancient tune which he had taught him. The sound was carried backwards by the wind, past the four smoking stacks. From an open window his grandfather sucked in the sound and offered a celtic prayer to the ancient Gods in thanksgiving for his grandson and for this opportunity to win his spirit. On his return to his cabin Benedict joined in conversation with his grandfather.

"Do you feel it?" asked the old man softly as he stared through the open window.

"No." replied the young man realising to ask feel what? would have been impertinent.

"The passing of many, here this night, to the otherworld."

"How will this be?"

The old priest didn't answer but after a while he said solemnly "You have been accepted by the unicorn."

Benedict knew enough of the old ways to realise that his grandfather had travelled to the otherworld on his behalf and seen the unicorn three times. This meant that he would be one of those to pass over this night. This scared Benedict, that is, it scared the modern side of him. He had seen his grandfather counsel many islanders and they had all departed this life peacefully. Now it was his turn, but he was not peaceful, he didn't want to leave this life, he was too young and had much to do. Sensing his troubled mind the celtic priest lay his hands onto his grandson and softly crafted his words. This had an instant calming effect and Benedict sank into a trance like state as he connected with his roots. Whilst in this state the old celtic priest reached for his bag and withdrew an old cutting tool. Opening the young man's shirt he cut the outline of a unicorn onto his chest, all the time softly chanting a celtic prayer.

The collision, when it came was a surprise to all except the two celts who remained in

their cabin lying on their twin beds, one old man, one young man, one old unicorn, one young unicorn. Both men remained serene as the shouts from the deck above grew louder as the ship tilted further forward. A loud knock on their cabin door was accompanied by a man's voice which shouted "All passengers to the boat deck, the ship is sinking."

Long after the noise in the corridor had subsided the two celts stirred and in silence made their unhurried way upwards to the boat deck. The scene was frantic. The last of the lifeboats was being hoisted and several deck hands were trying to restrain a rush of a dozen men trying to board it. A gunshot rang out. The rest of the deck was full of men, some standing in dignified silence, others were kneeling in prayer. A couple shouted obscenities and blasphemies, one against the Christian God, the other against the Hebrew God. The two celts were pushed from behind by two young men shouting "Make way, make way." as they struggled with an improvised raft. A choir was singing Nearer My God to Thee, accompanied by a string quartet, and then the sound of the bagpipes broke in playing a steady ghostlike sound that no-one could give a name to. The great ship tilted further, prompting more loud shouts of fear. The old celt removed his blue medallion and placed it around the neck of the young celt and then he plunged into the crowd leaving his grandson behind. As the lifeboats pulled away from the stricken ship one boat slowed its pace as an injured crew man tired. He was relieved by an old man in strange clothing who drew the oars with fresh

strength belying his age. No one remembered him getting aboard. As one of the passengers held up a lantern she saw a beautiful white unicorn which seemed to move over the old man's chest in time with his strokes. He didn't speak, his piercing blue eyes were fixed on the sinking wreck as he and the others listened in silence to the sound of the soft refrain of the pipes as it drifted across the ocean under a clear star lit sky. There were guttural cries from the survivors in the boats, as the mighty ship slipped under the surface, amid terrible rumblings of the giant's boilers exploding.

As the sea reverted to silence only the sound of the bagpipes could be heard once more playing the soft notes of a tune no-one knew. The choir and the string quartet had been silenced .The elderly woman who was sat facing the celtic priest raised her eyes from the galloping unicorn to look into the old man's eyes; she saw reflected there many golden lights slowly rising from the sea to the heavens. On turning she saw nothing, only the swelling sea. The old man stared passed her at the many souls departing to the otherworld, just like he had seen many souls arrive and depart all his life on his beloved island on the fringe of the Christian world.

The American senator put an advert in one of the New York newspapers asking if any-one who survived the Titanic disaster had come across an elderly Scott accompanied by his 19 year old grandson. He received one reply from an elderly English lady who told him what she saw.

Garret, the celtic priest, returned to the island without meeting the senator and without his grandson. He was warmly welcomed by the people including his son, Benedict's father.

Benedict was not mourned, his name was not even mentioned; his mother left the island for good a broken woman, bitter that she had lost her son to the old ways.

A year later, as Garret lay on his death bed, a young celtic priest arrived on the island. He had penetrating blue eyes which could see into one's soul. On his chest galloped a unicorn and around his neck he wore a pendant of blue stone set in pewter. His name was Benedict.

About the Author

Michael Trelissic, real name Michael McLarnon was born during the deep winter of 1946; a few months after the war in Europe had ended. Brought up in the industrial north of England by his widowed mother and his beloved grandmother his childhood was a happy one. After the death of his father when only six months old, his mother worked long hours as a paint sprayer in a firm of cabinet makers situated at the far end of the town. As a young boy he would often wait at the bus stop for her return. She would bring him waste offcuts of wood which his imagination turned into model bridges, castles and the like. He invented the first marble run in the mid 1950's, so much more intricate than the plastic versions you see today. He was devastated by the death of his mother at the young age of 55 from heart disease, no doubt brought on by the many years of exposure to lead paints and cigarette smoke. She and his grandmother, who had died a few years earlier, left him a legacy of unconditional love by which principal he has tried to live his life. Some of this is reflected in his latest novel, Sophia. As a child his playgrounds were the chemical dumps and contaminated fields which he shared with his best friend Rod and which his imagination had transformed into the much fabled green and pleasant lands of England.

Now, at the age of 77, macular degeneration is badly affecting his ability to see and therefore to write, but he continues as best he can with a little help from his friends.

His otherbooks include:

Sophia
Heron
Heron the sequel-due out in 2025
Fairy Tales for the Cynic
Tales of the Titanic
My Book of Profound Poems-due out 20925

Printed in Great Britain
by Amazon